Fact Finders®

MEDIA LITERACY

Music Madness

Questioning Music and Music Videos

by Neil Andersen

Capstone press®

Mankato, Minnesota

Fact Finders is published by Capstone Press,
151 Good Counsel Drive, P.O. Box 669, Mankato, Minnesota 56002.
www.capstonepress.com

Library of Congress Cataloging-in-Publication Data
Andersen, Neil.
  Music madness: questioning music and music videos / by Neil Andersen.
    p. cm.—(Fact Finders. Media literacy)
  Summary: "Describes what media is, how music and music videos are part of media, and encourages readers to question the medium's influential messages"—Provided by publisher.
  Includes bibliographical references and index.
  ISBN-13: 978-0-7368-6765-8 (hardcover)
  ISBN-10: 0-7368-6765-1 (hardcover)
  ISBN-13: 978-0-7368-7861-6 (softcover pbk.)
  ISBN-10: 0-7368-7861-0 (softcover pbk.)
  1. Popular music—Social aspects—Juvenile literature. 2. Music videos—Social aspects—Juvenile literature. [1. Popular music. 2. Music videos.] I. Title. II. Series.
ML3928.A48 2007
306.4'8424—dc22   2006023372

Editorial Credits
Jennifer Besel, editor; Juliette Peters, designer; Jo Miller, photo researcher/photo editor

Photo Credits
BigStock/winterberg, 3, 15, 20, 24 (background)
Capstone Press/Gary Sundermeyer, cover, 29 (CD); Karon Dubke, 4 (middle, right), 6 (left),
  7 (screen shots), 8 (top left, bottom two), 9 (all), 10 (top), 11 (top), 13 (CDs on left), 14 (all), 15, 16, 17 (all), 19, 21 (all), 22 (middle), 23 (bottom three), 24 (all), 25, 27 (all), 28 (top right), 29 (top right)
Corbis/Bettmann, 28 (top left); Neal Preston, 11 (middle); Nubar Alexanian, 22 (bottom); Penny
  Tweedie, 23 (top); Reuters/Lucas Jackson, 26 (bottom); Sygma/Robert Eric, 11 (bottom); zefa/Rainer Holz, 10 (bottom)
Courtesy of Neil Andersen, 32
FreeCovers.net, 6 (right), 7 (CD), 8 (top right), 12 (all), 13 (CDs on right), 18 (all), 20 (bottom), 22 (top),
  26 (top two), 29 (top left)
Getty Images Inc./DMI/Time Life Pictures, 20 (top); Hulton Archive, 28 (bottom); The Image
  Bank/Andersen Ross, 10 (second from top); Taxi/Peter Beavis, 10 (third from top)
Shutterstock/Ken Hurst, 4 (left); Marc Dietrich, cover (CD case); Perry Correll, cover (microphone)

1 2 3 4 5 6 12 11 10 09 08 07

TABLE OF CONTENTS

Medium Loud

What would you say if I told you that you use the **media** every day? Think I'm crazy? Take a look around. TV is a part of the media. Books are media. CDs are media too. Media is everywhere!

Different parts of the media come in many shapes and sizes. But the different forms of the media have two things in common. They all communicate a message and they all have the power to **influence** us.

The media, including music and music videos, tells us things about the world around us. But what we're told might not always be the entire story. That's why it's important to question media messages. Let's use these questions to see how music and music videos can influence us.

QUESTION IT!

Who made the message and why?

Who is the message for?

How might others view the message differently?

What is left out of the message?

How does the message get and keep my attention?

Words and Music By...

Who made the message and why?

You might think it's easy to know who made a song or video. The artist, right? But it's not that simple. Almost every CD you own came from a record label. RCA Label Group has a contract with Carrie Underwood. Kid Rock works with Atlantic Records. These companies manage the making, the marketing, and the selling of CDs. They get a big piece of the profits too.

"Listen to Me, Baby"

And that brings us to why labels and musicians make music. Many musicians record singles or CDs to express themselves. In 1984, Lee Greenwood (through MCA Records) released the patriotic song "God Bless the U.S.A." This song expresses Greenwood's love for his country and its military. He wanted the song to influence others to feel the same.

Money Machines

The main driving force in the music industry, though, is money. Not every song is a hit. But when a record goes platinum, labels and artists rake in the dough.

Labels do all they can to sell songs. Music videos and radio play can make all the difference. Basically, videos and radio play are commercials for a song. Labels and artists want to influence you to buy what they are selling.

Have you heard the songs on these platinum albums?

LINGO

platinum: when more than 1 million copies of an album are sold

product placement: putting products and logos in music or videos so people will hear about them or see them

Britney Spears' video "Baby One More Time" was an instant hit, which helped make her CD a hit too.

Musical Commercials

Product placement is another way artists make money through their music. Some artists actually put ads for products in their songs. A research project called American Brandstand tracks product placements in songs. In 2004, it found that Kanye West dropped in 19 placements in his four singles. Do you think ads in songs affect you?

Product placements in videos are so common you probably don't even realize they're there. Ciara's video "1, 2 Step" highlights Axe body spray. Product placements like that are easy to miss. But look closely next time you watch VH1 or MTV. You might be surprised by what those videos are trying to influence you to buy.

It takes a whole lot of people to pull together a hit record and a great video. Here's a little behind-the-scenes info.

The **PRODUCER** makes sure the recording or video production stays on budget and on time. She's pretty much the boss of the team.

The **RECORDING ENGINEER** uses recording equipment to record the musicians. Without him, we wouldn't have much to listen to.

The **MUSICIANS** are the people who get the most fame. They are the people we buy concert tickets to see.

The **A&R SCOUT** works for a record label. He signs new talent to work with the company.

The **MUSIC VIDEO DIRECTOR** develops the treatment for the video. She runs the show when the shooting begins.

The **DIRECTOR OF PHOTOGRAPHY** takes care of the camera angles. It's his job to get the shots the director needs.

The **EDITOR** pieces together all the parts after the video has been shot. Using editing equipment, he makes the video look like what we see on TV.

Who is the message for?

Years ago, music on the radio was meant for everyone. The rich voices of Frank Sinatra, Bing Crosby, and Ella Fitzgerald filled the airwaves. The lyrics appealed to a large general audience.

But today, different styles of music, from country to hip-hop, blare from our speakers. Artists and record companies know that not every kind of music appeals to every kind of person. So they target their music to specific audiences. Take hip-hop, for example. Many rap songs describe the joys and sorrows of inner-city life. These types of songs appeal to an audience that can relate to the situations.

Tuning In

Radio stations help record companies reach target audiences. They do this by having specific **formats**. A country music station plays only country music. They do this so country music lovers will tune in. And, hopefully, hearing a song many times on the radio will make you want to download the MP3.

TRY IT OUT!

In order to make more money, some companies make **compilation** CDs that target certain audiences. You can make your own compilation. Grab your CDs and get to work.

- First, pick your target audience. Think about what your target audience likes in music.
- Now pick out 10 songs your audience will like.
- Make a list of the songs you chose.

When you're done, have someone from your target audience listen to the songs on your list. Did they like your compilation? Why or why not?

My Music on TV

Artists and record companies play their music and videos where their target audience will be. They know better than to waste time and money putting a country song on a rap station. That's why TV networks that play videos also have specific formats. Videos shown on BET are meant to appeal to an African American audience. CMT hopes to draw in country fans. Record companies hope viewers will like what they see and hear enough to buy the song.

Compare these two video shots. Can you tell just by looking at them who their target audiences are?

REALITY CHECK

MySpace is a popular place for bands to target a specific audience. Most MySpace users are 18 to 34 years old and are looking for new and different music.

In 2005, the band Arctic Monkeys saw an opportunity. They created a site on MySpace. They posted their songs there and let people hear them for free. The Arctic Monkeys became famous as more and more people heard the band's music. A major label signed the band because of its online marketing success. Many people thought that no one would buy the band's CDs since their songs could be heard for free. But they were wrong. Why do you think people bought the band's music even though it was on MySpace?

Lyrics [Featuring Values]

How might others view this message differently?

Music is powerful. A song can make one person cry and make someone else laugh. But why? It's all about values. What we believe is important makes up our set of values. No one has the same values. Life experiences, age, gender, and religious beliefs affect our values. That's why you might think a Beyoncé song is great, but your mom thinks it sends the wrong kind of message.

TRY IT OUT!

Many hip-hop songs have lyrics that **promote** a value. You can try it out. Create a rhyme that you could rap to a good beat. In that rhyme, promote one or more of your own values. Here are some questions to help you get started.

- What do you love?
- What do you believe in?
- What do you hate?
- What would you like to influence people to do?

Use the answers to one or more of these questions in your rhyme.

Musical Values

Music lyrics and video images send us messages to try to make us think or act a certain way. Look at the video "Stupid Girls" by Pink. In the song, Pink says, "What happened to the dream of a girl president? She's dancing in the video next to 50 Cent." This song and video spread a powerful value. Pink makes fun of girls who act dumb to get a guy.

Values are everywhere in music. Listen to Natasha Bedingfield's song "Single." Can you pick out values in that song? Here are some of the lyrics. "I'm not waiting around for a man to save me. 'Cause I'm happy where I am. Don't depend on a guy to validate me."

The cool thing about music is that you can choose to be influenced or not. That's why questioning what you see and hear is so helpful.

"You Don't Know Everything"

What is left out of the message?

Music is everywhere. We're always hearing about love stories, break-ups, life on the streets, and how we should live our lives. But have you thought that maybe these songs aren't telling the whole story?

Questioning Violence

Violence is a part of many hip-hop songs. 50 Cent has based many of his songs on surviving gunshot wounds. But what his message leaves out is that many other people don't survive. Some listeners never question what they hear. They start to think that violence is the best way to solve problems. But we know that's not true, and that's why we question.

Stereotypes

Some music lyrics and videos also promote **stereotypes**. Black men play the "gangsta" much of the time. Does that mean that all African American guys are mean and violent? No way!

The truth is, music only gives us a small piece of information. There's a lot of other info that was left out. We have to question what we see and hear because the music doesn't always sing the whole story.

The video "We In Here" by DMX shows the tough-guy stereotype. Do you think videos like this make you think a certain way about African Americans?

REALITY CHECK

Record labels want to make as much money as possible. Sometimes they use tricks to do that. And sometimes those tricks go a little too far.

In 1988, the group Milli Vanilli released its album *All or Nothing*. The album was a hit. But there was something listeners didn't know. The men who were on stage and on the CD cover weren't the singers. You see, the label Arista liked the music of Charles Shaw, Johnny Davis, and Brad Howell. But they didn't think the group's image would appeal to the target audience. The label hired 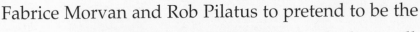 Fabrice Morvan and Rob Pilatus to pretend to be the group. The trick worked so well that Milli Vanilli even won a Grammy.

In November 1990, the scam was revealed. It only proved how much info we might be missing.

The U.S.-Remix Album
ALL OR NOTHING
including 4 new tracks

No. 1 in USA

Body Image

Many music videos show men watching beautiful women who are wearing skimpy clothes. The lyrics talk about how perfect bodies get a man's attention. This message leaves out the fact that most women don't look quite like the ones in the video. If you let videos and lyrics influence you, you would be missing a lot of information.

Check out Shakira's song "Hips Don't Lie" or Chris Brown's video "Yo (Excuse Me Miss)" and look at the way the women dress and move. Do they look like the women you see every day?

Produced by A-Ten-Shun Studios

How does the message get and keep my attention?

There are tons of artists who want to make it big. But in order for artists and record companies to make any money, they have to get your attention.

CD Covers

The way a CD is packaged can totally change what people think of an album. Record companies and artists pay special attention to CD covers. They want the covers to attract the target audience.

TV

TV is a great place to get people's attention. Playing gigs on shows like *The Tonight Show* and *SNL* help listeners put a face with a song.

Radio Play

Having a song played on the radio is a great way to get attention. If stations play the song in heavy **rotation**, more people will hear it. And hopefully, they'll want to buy it.

Music Videos

Ever notice that music videos jump around a lot? They go from scene to scene, then back again. Those jumps are called quick cuts. Video makers use this jolting technique to keep you interested.

Fancy sets and beautiful people are also used to get your attention. Do you think some videos use violence to get your heart pumping?

Bo Bice's video "The Real Thing" uses quite a few quick cuts. Next time it's on, pay attention to how it keeps you interested.

LINGO

gig: a concert

quick cut: fast scene changes that are meant to jolt and excite you

23

REALITY CHECK

CD covers are meant to get attention. But record companies don't want to get the wrong kind of attention.

In 1968, the Rolling Stones released their album *Beggars Banquet*. The original cover showed writing on a bathroom wall. But people complained that the cover was offensive. Making people upset isn't a good way to get them to buy your product. So the record company changed the cover to represent the values of the time.

Today, some people think CD covers are art. And that having to change a cover is **censorship**. What do you think?

replacement cover

Compare the original *Beggars Banquet* cover to CD covers you see today. Chances are you don't think this cover is so bad. That's because values are different today than they were in the 1960s.

Musically Speaking

Let's talk about the actual music for a second. Songwriters know that a song must be catchy if they want people to buy it. That's why most songs have what's called a hook. A hook is a catchy phrase that's repeated throughout the song. It's the part you find yourself singing in the shower. Listen to Kelly Clarkson's hit "Walk Away." What do you think the hook is? Hint: It starts "I'm lookin' for attention..."

TRY IT OUT!

Design a CD cover for the compilation of songs you made earlier. Remember to think about what your target audience likes. Here are some questions to help get you started.

- What kinds of things does the target audience like to do?
- What does the target audience wear?
- Does the target audience use any special or unique words?

Use the answers to these questions to design your cover.

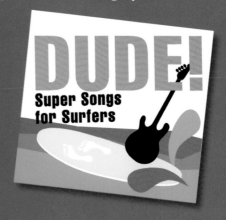

DUDE! Super Songs for Surfers

Keepin' Ya Hooked

Once a band has your attention, they have to keep it. If they don't, you might not buy their music. Hidden tracks are a fun way to keep listeners. On some CDs, bands will place a song on a track way after the last regular song. These hidden tracks aren't advertised. Bands rely on word of mouth to spread the word.

Even really popular bands like Sublime and The Black Eyed Peas put hidden tracks on their discs.

Concert tours are a huge way to keep people interested. Tours are hard work for the artists and their crew. But it's a great way to keep fans wanting more.

Question the Sweet Sounds

Music is a huge part of our lives. It can pump you up or calm you down. It can also influence your thoughts and actions—but only if you let it. So grab your CD case, pop one in the player, and have fun questioning the music.

Time Line

Guglielmo Marconi sends and receives the first radio signals, beginning the use of radio.

The Rolling Stones' cover for their album *Beggars Banquet* is changed. This just showed how record companies respond to people's values.

1895   1920   1968   1981

KDKA, the first commercial radio station, goes on the air in Pittsburgh.

MTV broadcasts the first music video, "Video Killed the Radio Star."

The Milli Vanilli scam is revealed, proving that record labels go to great lengths to attract an audience.

The Arctic Monkeys create a site on MySpace, allowing them to easily reach their target audience.

1983　　**1990**　　**1996**　　**2005**

CD technology is introduced in the United States.

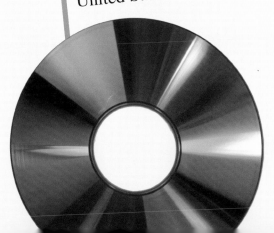

The MP3 player gets a U.S. patent.

GLOSSARY

censorship (SEN-sur-ship)—the removal of something that is thought to be harmful or offensive to the public

compilation (kom-puh-LAY-shun)—a list or other grouping of information from many sources

format (FOR-mat)—the shape or style of something

influence (IN-floo-uhnss)—to have an effect on someone or something

media (MEE-dee-uh)—a group of mediums that communicates messages; one piece of the media, like music or music videos, is called a medium.

promote (pruh-MOTE)—to make the public aware of something or someone

rotation (roh-TAY-shuhn)—the order music and videos are played; heavy rotation means a song or video is played more than other songs or videos.

stereotype (STER-ee-oh-tipe)—an overly simple opinion of a person, group, or thing

INTERNET SITES

FactHound offers a safe, fun way to find Internet sites related to this book. All of the sites on FactHound have been researched by our staff.

Here's how:

1. Visit *www.facthound.com*

2. Choose your grade level.

3. Type in this book ID **0736867651** for age-appropriate sites. You may also browse subjects by clicking on letters, or by clicking on pictures and words.

4. Click on the **Fetch It** button.

FactHound will fetch the best sites for you!

READ MORE

Ali, Dominic. *Media Madness: An Insider's Guide to Media.* Tonawanda, N.Y.: Kids Can Press, 2005.

Cefrey, Holly. *Backstage at a Music Video*. Backstage Pass. New York: Children's Press, 2003.

INDEX

MEET THE AUTHOR

Neil Andersen's interest in the media has led him to a career teaching others about it. Neil is an executive member of the Association for Media Literacy and serves on the board of the Media-Awareness Network. In addition to working as the media literacy consultant for the Toronto District School Board, he gives presentations and workshops worldwide.